W. Lepard

The history and the mystery of Good-Friday

The fifth edition

W. Lepard

The history and the mystery of Good-Friday
The fifth edition

ISBN/EAN: 9783741197697

Manufactured in Europe, USA, Canada, Australia, Japa

Cover: Foto ©Andreas Hilbeck / pixelio.de

Manufactured and distributed by brebook publishing software
(www.brebook.com)

W. Lepard

The history and the mystery of Good-Friday

THE

HISTORY

AND THE

MYSTERY

OF

GOOD-FRIDAY.

The FIFTH EDITION.

LONDON:

Printed for W. LEPARD, Newgate-Street, and
J. BUCKLAND, Paternoster-Row.

M DCC LXXXII.

[Price One Shilling.]

GOOD-FRIDAY.

IT has always been accounted good policy in the church of Rome to withhold the Holy Scriptures from the laity, and to perform the public worſhip of Almighty God in Latin, a language unknown to the people. A religion founded on the infallible judgment of one man, and requiring of all the reſt of mankind an abſolute ſubmiſſion to his dictates, ought not to be examined; for, ſhould the people emerge from credulity, and riſe into reaſon and faith, the bold Pretender to Infallibility would tumble from the pinnacle of pontifical dignity into a gulf of univerſal contempt.

That wiſe and vigorous ſet of men, the Proteſtant Reformers, broke open the papal cabinet, expoſed his pretended titles to public view, and did all in their power to ſimplify religion, and to reduce it to its original plainneſs and purity.

They

They laid open the infpired writings, they taught the right of private judgment, and they fummoned all mankind to enter into that liberty with which Jefus Chrift had made them free.

If thefe men had a fault, it lay in the breadth of their fcale; they aimed to convert whole nations at once, and to change their cuftoms in a day. Many religious cuftoms were incorporated with civil rights, it was irreligion in ecclefiaftics to exercife civil government, and it became therefore effential to the accomplifhment of their plan to call in the aid of fecular powers. Secular powers readily affifted them; but at the fame time obliged them to keep meafures with royal prerogatives, court factions, the intrigues of the old clergy, and the prejudices of the common people. They therefore left the reformation unfinifhed, and died in hopes that their fucceffors would complete in happier periods what they had begun. Far from entering into this juft and liberal defign, we feem to have loft fight of it, and to have adopted principles fubverfive of the whole. We feem to have difcarded piety, incorporated luxury, and the few who have not given up all fenfe of fhame, endeavour to conceal the fcandal under a cover of fuperftition. Thus we affect modefty, and dance naked in a net to hide our fhame!

2   Super-

Superftition is to religion, fays one, what aftrology is to aftronomy, the foolifh daughter of a wife mother. Thefe two have long fubjugated mankind. We have no objection in general againft days of fafting and prayer, they have always the advantage of retaining a fcriptural form of godlinefs, they are often edifying, and fometimes neceffary. Nor do we find fault with thofe Chriftians who make confcience of obferving all the feftivals of their own churches. They have a right to judge for themfelves, and their fincerity will be rewarded. Neither will we fuppofe the Englifh clergy to have been deficient in teaching their people, that all practical religion divides into the two parts of moral obligations, and pofitive inftitutes; that the firft are univerfal, unalterable, and eternal; and that the laft were appointed by legiflature to ferve the purpofes of the firft. But as the caufe of moral rectitude can never be pleaded too often, nor the nature of it explained too clearly, as fuperftition is very apt to invade the rights of religion, and as numbers who have great intereft in thefe articles have not leifure to trace them through folios, it may not be unfeafonble, and we truft it will not be deemed impertinent, to expofe to public view in brief the hiftory—the authority—the piety—and the polity of church

holi-

holidays. To difcufs one is to examine all, and we felect for this purpofe that day, on which, it is reputed, the founder of our holy religion was crucified, commonly called Good-Friday.

The History of Good-Friday.

Let no one blame an hiftorian who does not begin before his records, it is not his fault, it is his virtue. Strictly fpeaking, all documents in Proteftant churches fhould be found in the holy canon ; for the people of each church refer an inquifitive man to their clergy, their clergy refer him to their printed confeffions of faith, and all their confeffions refer him to Scripture. There are many ceremonies in fome Proteftant churches which do not pretend to derive themfelves from Scripture immediately, but they were appointed, they fay, by thofe who were appointed by Scripture to ordain them. The examination of this appointment does not fall under this article, and we defer it to the next. At prefent we only obferve, Good-Friday is a ceremony of this kind, and the original records of pure Chriftianity fay nothing about it.

Neither any one Evangelift, nor all the four together, narrate the *whole* hiftory of Jefus Chrift, nor yet *all* the circumftances of thofe

parts

parts on which they enlarge moſt. St. John, the laſt of theſe hiſtorians, cloſes his hiſtory with a declaration, that *many things* relative to Jeſus Chriſt were *not written.* The times of the birth and crucifixion of our Saviour are ſo written in theſe authentic records, that nothing certain can be determined concerning them. All who have pretended to ſettle theſe periods are conjecturers, and not hiſtorians, as their variety proves. There is only one opinion in the whole Chriſtian world concerning the country of Jeſus Chriſt, and the place of his nativity; all allow he was a Jew, and born at Bethlehem. We ſhould be equally uniform in our belief of the times of his birth and crucifixion, had Scripture as clearly determined the laſt as it has related the firſt. There are more than one hundred and thirty opinions concerning the *year* of his nativity, and the *day* of it has been placed by men of equal learning in every month of the year. There is a like variety of opinions concerning the time of his crucifixion. Let us reſpect the ſilence of the oracles of God. No argument can be drawn from it to endanger Chriſtianity. A point of chronology is not an object of ſaving faith, nor is zeal for an undecided queſtion any part of that holineſs, without which none ſhall ſee the Lord. The inſpired

writers

writers did not defign to make laws about feafts, but to enforce the practice of piety and virtue.

The firft congregations of Chriftians confifted of native Jews, Jewifh profelites, and Pagans of different countries, and of divers fects. Each clafs brought into the Chriftian church fome of their old education prejudices, and endeavoured to incorporate them with the doctrine and worfhip of Chriftianity. The Apoftles guarded againft this unnatural union, and, during their lives, prevented the profeffion of it; but after their deceafe they were made to coalefce, and from this coalition came Good-Friday, and other church holidays. Chriftianity affirmed the facts —profelite mathematicians gueffed at the times— pretended fcholars accommodated prophecy and hiftory to the favourite periods—and devotional men, whofe whole knowledge confifted in an art of turning popular notions to pious purpofes, began to obferve the days themfelves, by the aufterity of their examples they gave them a fanctimonious air to others, and fo recommended them to the obfervation of all who chofe to be accounted pious as well as wife.

We hear nothing of Eafter till the fecond century, and then we find Polycarp, Anicetus, and others conferring on the time of keeping it, celebrating it at different times, and exercifing a
mutual

mutual toleration notwithstanding their differences. Jesus Christ was crucified at the time of the Jewish passover. The Christians of Asia celebrated Easter on the *fourteenth* day of the moon, according to the law of Moses, on whatever day of the week it fell, so that if they kept some years a Good *Friday*, they also kept in other years Good *Monday*, Good *Saturday*, or Good *any* day, for the day of Christ's crucifixion must be at its due distance from the day of his resurrection. These Eastern Christians pretended St. John kept Easter so. The western churches used to observe the *Sunday* after the fourteenth day of the March moon, and they said St. Peter and St. Paul always did so. If these Christians could not convince one another in times so near those of the Apostles, it is not likely we should be able to determine the time of Easter now. We have nothing more then to add here, except that they debated and differed like Christians, they tolerated one another, they communicated together, and the liberal temper of such disputants is always edifying, however idle we may think the dispute.

About the year 190 Victor I. then bishop of the church at Rome, had the audacity to excommunicate those Christians who kept Easter on the fourteenth day of the moon. The excommunicated

communicated pitied his pride, and persevered
in their practice. The Roman bishops intrigued,
caballed, got councils called, and at length the
council of Arles, held in the year 314, having
no doubt the fear of God before their eyes, and
being endued with more wisdom, more power,
or more presumption than their predecessors,
DECREED that *all* churches should celebrate Easter
on the *Sunday* after the fourteenth of the moon
of March, when that moon should happen after
the vernal equinox. Eleven years after, the
council of Nice confirmed this decree, and the
Emperor Constantine enforced it by orders sent
into all the provinces of the empire. The council did not think to provide for one difficulty
which might arise, which might produce a new
dissention, and throw down that idol, *uniformity*,
which these Christian Nebuchadnezzars had committed so many crimes to set up. The fourteenth
day of the full moon in March might fall on a
Sunday. It did so. A difficulty started, and
different opinions followed. The Eastern churches
celebrated Easter on the day of the full moon,
when it fell on a Sunday in March. The western Christians deferred it to the Sunday fol-
lowing. How could a synod of 318 bishops,
they were but men, foresee this difficulty!

In

In the seventh century, one of our petty kings, Ofwy, having been instructed in the Christian religion by Scotch Monks, kept Easter after the Asian fashion, while his queen, who had been taught by a Roman priest, observed it in the western way; and it sometimes happened, that his majesty was joyfully celebrating our Saviour's resurrection, while the queen was fasting on account of his crucifixion. To get rid of this inconvenience, the king summoned a council to meet at Withby to determine the original time of Easter. The clergy on the one side rested their cause on tradition derived from St. John, while the clergy on the other urged that which came from St. Peter. The king was judge, the balance inclined neither way, and long was he perplexed with authorities quite equal, at length being informed, that, however great St. John might be, St. Peter kept *the keys* of the kingdom of heaven, the king very prudently took care of the main chance, declared for St. Peter, and Easter has fallen on a Sunday in England ever since.

Good-Friday had the fate of all other holidays, it had a solemn service composed for it, and, being established by civil power, the people were obliged to fast—and to pray—and to say—and to sing—and so on to the end of the chapter.

B   When

When king Henry VIII. reformed the British church, although he difcarded many feftivals, yet he thought proper to retain Eafter, and Lent its appendage. The old fervice was afterwards new vamped, and during the fucceeding reigns of Elizabeth and the Stuarts many were perfecuted for refufing to comply with it. That ineftimable prince, William III. procured a toleration, the prefent auguft family protect it, and the inhabitants of this country now enjoy the liberty of keeping feftivals, or of renouncing them.

The hiftory then in brief is this. Neither Good-Friday, nor any other Fafts or Feafts were appointed to be obferved by the Lord Jefus Chrift, or his apoftles. The time of Chrift's birth cannot be made out, and that of his crucifixion is uncertain. Could we affure ourfelves of the year, we could not prove that the Jews obferved the regreffions of the equinox, nor that they made ufe of accurate aftronomical tables. No traces of Eafter are to be found in the firft century, nor for a great part of the fecond. When the firft obfervers of it appeared, they could not make evidence of their coming honeftly by it. Councils decreed that it fhould not be kept before the 21ft of March, nor after the 20th of April. Some, however, kept it on the 22d

of

of April, while others celebrated it on the 25th of March; others at times different from both, and others kept no day at all. Our anceſtors murdered one another for variety of opinion on this ſubject: but we are fallen under wiſer and better civil governors, who allow us to think and act as we pleaſe, provided the ſtate receives no detriment; ſo that the language of Scripture is ſpoken by the law of our country, *He who regardeth a day, let him regard it to the Lord: and he, who regardeth not a day, to the Lord let him not regard it.* What good chriſtian can refuſe to add a hearty Amen!

The AUTHORITY of *Good-Friday.*

Dull and uninteresting as this poor ſubject may be as an article of hiſtory, it becomes extremely important, when it is foiſted into the religion of Jeſus Chriſt, enjoined on all chriſtian people under pain of his diſpleaſure, and conſidered as the livery of loyalty and piety. In ſuch a caſe, the diſciples of the Son of God are compelled to enquire, whoſe are we, and whom do we ſerve? His we are whom we obey.

Should a man from an idea of the chriſtian church from reading the New Teſtament, in which Jewiſh ceremonies are ſaid to be a yoke,

which

which neither the Jews of Chrift's time, nor their anceftors were able to bear—in which thofe rites are called weak and beggarly elements—rudiments of the world—fhadows of good things to come, of which Jefus Chrift was the fubftance—and fhould he then behold a chriftian church loaded with ceremonies of pagan and Jewifh extraction, there would naturally arife a violent prejudice in his mind againft this modern church, and he would be obliged to enquire what Joab had a hand in this alteration.

' It muft be allowed, confummate wifdom—cool and unbiaffed judgment—rectitude the moft rigid—and benevolence and power the moft extenfive, are abfolutely and indifpenfably neceffary qualifications in religious legiflation. The nature of God and Man—the relation of each to the other—and of both to all the countlefs conditions and circumftances of all the reft of mankind—the kind of worfhip—and the manner of performing it—the neceffary requifitions of juftice—and the proper effufions of goodnefs—with a thoufand other articles from one grand complex whole, which would baffle all, except infinite penetration, in forming a fyftem of real religion.

' As an affumption of legiflative power in religion is an afcent to the moft elevated degree of
honour,

honour, and as it requires a kind of fubmiffion to which human dignity is loth to bow, fo, it muft be fuppofed, the cleareft evidence of a right to exercife it is naturally expected. No blind fubmiffion—no precarious titles—no fpurious records—no popular clamour—nothing but clear revelation expounded by accurate reafoning can be taken in evidence here. An immortal intelligence is the nobleft production of infinite power and fkill—when it pays its homage to the Deity it is in its nobleft exercife—and no mean guide muft conduct fuch a being then.

On thefe juft principles I take up Good-Friday where I find it, as part of the eftablifhed religion of my country, and I modeftly enquire the authority that made it fo. A few old women refer me to the fourth verfe of the twelfth of Acts for the word *Eafter*, and I return the compliment by referring them to their grandfons at fchool, who fay St. Luke wrote *paffover*. I could, were I inclined to revenge, be even with thefe old ladies by telling the tale of Lady Eafter, Afhtar, or Afhtaroth, a Sidonian toaft : but I am too bufy and too placid now, and I take my leave of this goddefs, and alfo of the godly tranflator, who profaned a Jewifh faft by nick-naming it after a pagan proftitute, and laid the blame on innocent St. Luke.

The

The established clergy do not pretend to support their festivals by authority of Scripture: but they say their legal authority arises from that act of parliament, which ratified the thirty-nine articles of their faith, one of which affirms, *the* CHURCH *hath power to decree rites and ceremonies, and authority in controversies of faith.* This clause is said by them to mean, that the " governors of the church have power to determine what shall be received and professed for *truth* among the members of the church, and to bind them to *submission* to their sentence, though they err in their sentence." These are their own words.

These thirty-nine articles were first produced in a convocation of the clergy in the year 1562— they were reviewed by another convocation in 1571—and were afterwards ratified by parliament. It is an unquestionable fact, that the religion of all the good people of the church of England was, in 1562, put to the vote of one hundred and seventeen priests, many of whom could hardly write their names, and several of whom were not present, and voted by proxy, and that ceremonies and holidays were carried by a majority of *one* single vote, and that given by proxy. Whether the absent member, who had the casting vote, were talking, or journeying, or hunting, or sleeping, is immaterial, he

was

was the god almighty of this article of Englifh religion, and his power decreed rites and ceremonies and matters of *high beheft*.

The infertion of the above claufe of the CHURCH's *power* in the twentieth article was an infamous piece of prieftcraft. It is not in king Edward's articles. It is not in the original manufcripts fubfcribed by the convocation, and ftill preferved in Bennet College, Cambridge, among the papers of Bifhop Parker, who was prefident of the affembly—It was not in the printed book ratified by parliament—It was not in the latin tranflations of thofe times—nor did it dare to fhew itfclf till twenty-two years after, as Heylin, and other high churchmen allow.

Subfcription to this claufe is mere mummery; for what does it mean? The *church* power to decree rites and ceremonies! An abfolute falfehood. One perfon in this church, and one perfon only hath power to decree rites and ceremonies. The common people pretend to none. The clergy have introduced organs—pictures—candles on the communion table—bowing towards the eaft—and placing the communion table altar-wife: but they had no right to do fo; for as the Common Prayer book no where enjoins them, they are exprefsly prohibited by the act of uniformity, which fays no rites or

ceremonies

ceremonies ſhall be uſed in any church - - - other
than what is preſcribed and APPOINTED to be
uſed in and by the Common Prayer book. By
what effrontery does a prieſt allow organs in publick worſhip after he has ſubſcribed to the truth
of an homily, which declares them ſuperſtitious!
Or with what preſumption does he dare, in direct oppoſition to act of parliament, to invade a
prerogative that belongs to the crown! Neither
a convocation, nor an houſe of commons, nor a
houſe of lords, nor all together have a power to
decree rites, ceremonies, and articles of faith in
the eſtabliſhed church of England, the conſtitution
has confirmed it as a royal prerogative, and annexed it to the imperial crown of this realm.

In former times our kings ceded this prerogative to the pope, at the Reformation they re-claim-
ed it, and long after the Reformation they refuſed
to ſuffer the other branches of the legiſlature to
examine, or to meddle with it : but in later
times this prerogative was bounded, and now it
is reſtrained to the national eſtabliſhed church.
By the act of toleration the crown agreed to reſign, and in effect it did actually reſign this prerogative in regard to the Nonconformiſts, and
this ceſſion is become a part of the conſtitution
by the authority of the whole legiſlative power
of the Britiſh empire. The mode of reſtraint,
indeed

indeed, is not fo explicit as it might have been; but the fact is undeniable.

The Englifh Nonconformifts think *civil government* natural, neceffary, and of divine appointment—they fuppofe the *form* of it arbitrary, and left to the free choice of all nations under heaven—they believe the form of *mixt monarchy* to be the beft—but were they in Venice they would yield *civil* obedience to ariftocracy; in Holland to a republic, or in France to an abfolute monarchy, the beft mode of civil government making no part of their religion—They think in all ftates impliedly, and in the Britifh moft exprefsly, there fubfifts an *original contract* between the prince and the people—they believe the *limitation* of regal prerogative by bounds fo certain that it is impoffible a prince fhould ever exceed them without the confent of the people, one of the principal bulwarks of civil liberty—they think there are *ordinary* courfes of law clearly eftablifhed, and not to be difobeyed, and they believe there are *extraordinary* recourfes to fixt principles neceffary when the contracts of fociety are in danger of diffolution—they think thefe principles alone are the *bafes* of prerogative and liberty, of the king's title to the crown, and that freedom which they enjoy under his aufpicious reign; and thefe, their fentiments,

C   are

are thofe of the wifeft philofophers—the ableft lawyers—and the moft accomplifhed ftatefmen, that Britain ever produced.

The Englifh Nonconformifts abfolutely deny all *human* authority in matters of religion—they deny it to *all* civil governments of every form —they think Jefus Chrift the *fole head* of the Chriftian church—they fay the *Scriptures* are his only code of confcience law—All the articles of their belief are contained in *his* doctrine—all their hopes of obtaining immortal felicity in *his* mediation—all their moral duties in the great law of nature explained by *revelation*—and all their religious rites, and ecclefiaftical law in *his* pofitive inftitutes unexplained, or rather unperplexed by human creeds—they fay Jefus Chrift himfelf does not require obedience *without evidence*—that they fubmit to him, *as God gave him*, as a prophet, a prieft, and a king, on the fulleft proof—they fay their religion has nothing hoftile to *civil government*, but is highly beneficial to it—that although it is no part of it to determine the beft form, yet it is a part of it to fubmit in civil matters to the powers that be. On thefe principles they juftify the apoftles for embracing Chriftianity, when religious governors rejected it—the firft miffionaries, who fubverted eftablifhed religions by propagating it—
the

the reformation from popery—and therevolution, that dethroned high church tyranny. For their civil principles they are ready to die as *Britons*, and for their religious ones as *Chriftians*.

But we have loft *Friday!*—no wonder. Good-Friday is a rebel againft the king of kings, and always when loyal fubjects approach him the traitor lurks behind, fkulks among popes and priefts, and hides his guilty head in a cowl, muttering—*the church hath power to decree rites and ceremonies.* Ah Sirrah!

The article of authority, then, amounts to this. In that fyftem of religion, which goes on the principles of the perfection and fufficiency of Scripture, and the fole legiflation of Jefus Chrift, Church-holidays are non-entities. In thofe fyftems, which allow human authority, they reft on the power that appoints them. In this happy country the power that appoints them, is conftitutionally bounded, and has agreed to fpend its force on as many as choofe to fubmit to it, and to exert itfelf againft all who dare to impede, who choofe to renounce it. So that the authority, which appoints a Good-Friday ceremonial, has juft as much influence over a Britifh fubject, as he himfelf choofes to give it. If he choofe to be a member of the national church, to which certainly there are many wordly in-

C 2   ducements,

ducements, he allows human authority over conscience, and he ought in conscience (if it be possible for conscience to agree to its own dissolution) to keep the fast: but if he think proper to dissent, to which certainly there are strong religious inducements, he is protected in disowning the authority, and the obligation is void. When human wisdom affects to adorn a religion of divine revelation, it presumes to paint a diamond, or to lace and embroider the seamless coat of one, whose simplicity is his evidence and his church's glory. When such as Austin and Gregory, primitive manufacturers of trumpery, imported their bales, and offered their wares to the British church, they were objects of pity or contempt; but when they presumed to use coercive measures to make the denizens of heaven purchase their trash; when a pope like Judas came in the night with halberds, and swords, and staves; when, worse than he, the traitor did not bring even a lanthorn to enable men to read his commission—Merciful God! couldst thou be angry with our ancestors, for hand-cuffing the felon, and whipping him out of their isle! The punishment was too little for the crime. They should have burnt even his rags with fire!

The

The fury fiend with many a felon-deed,
Had ſtirr'd up mickle miſchievous deſpight.

The PIETY of Good-Friday.

If piety be the diſcharge of duty towards God, there are only two ſhort queſtions to anſwer. Firſt, is the obſervation of an annual faſt in commemoration of the death of Chriſt, a *duty* required by almighty God? Next, how is this duty *diſcharged* by thoſe, who think it a duty?

All duties, which God-requires of all mankind, are contained in the moral law. Moral obligations are founded in the nature and fitneſs of things. There is a fitneſs between the care of a parent, and the obedience of a child. Filial obedience is therefore a moral duty. There is a fitneſs between civil government and taxes. Governors protect ſubjects, and ſubjects ought therefore to ſupport governors. Taxes for the neceſſary ſupport of government are therefore dues, and the payment of them moral obligation. But nobody ever yet pretended to make the celebration of Eaſter a part of the moral law.

The other claſs of duties required of all Chriſtians is contained in poſitive inſtitutes. Baptiſm is a poſitive inſtitute; the celebration of the Lord's ſupper is a poſitive inſtitute. They would

not

not have been obligatory, they would not have
been known, had not the Chriftian legiflator in-
ftituted them; and they are obeyed now they
are appointed in proper fubmiffion to his authority. But has he appointed this faft? Does it
not wander about a mere beggar actually deftitute
of every token of a legitimate divine inftitute?

Since, then, the obfervation of this day is no
part of piety, we are driven, for want of mate-
rials to fill up this article in decent guife, to the
fad neceffity of turning the tables, and of confi-
dering the *impiety* of this black, this bloody Friday. Were we to collect into one aggregate
fum the impious actions that belong to the in-
troduction, the eftablifhment, the fupport of
ceremonies, one of which is this day; were we
to balance accounts between moral law and human inftitute, we fhould be obliged to charge to
the latter a moft enormous and ruinous fum.
We fhould fet down the unwarrantable implica-
tion of the imperfection of Chriftianity as Jefus
Chrift appointed it—the incorrigible obftinacy
of judaizing bunglers, who united a provincial
ritual with an univerfal religion—the rafh enter-
terprizes of minute philofophers, who affociated
the mummeries of Belial with the miracles of
Chrift—the paltry babbling of traditionifts, whofe
impertinence put them on pretending to give

6   evidence

evidence to wife and grave men by their fenfe-
lcfs repetitions of, I heard fay, that he heard fay,
that fhe heard fay, that they heard fay—the felf-
employed and uncommiffioned racket of councils—the daring atchievements of thofe knights
errant the popes of Rome—the bafe conceffions
and felf-contradictions of their hierarchical fquires
—their flattering, betraying, befooling, defert-
ing, and affaffinating emperors and kings—the
fubverting of all found maxims of civil polity,
every dictate of right reafon, the facred bonds
of fociety and the natural rights of mankind—
the degrading of magiftracy, the banifhment of
thoufands, the bloodfhedding . . . . . (O where
fhall we end?) . . . . All thefe under a mafk of
hypocrify,—a pious pretence of uniformity—the
erection of *a godlye order, in Chriften ftates amonge*
the holye flock that Iefu boughte with hys owne
bloode! I know I fhall be reputed a filly enthufiaft
for what I am going to fay; but what care I?
When the bells chime to call people to celebrate
Good-Friday, methinks they fay to me, *count*
the coft . . . . *thinking Chriftian, count the coft*—I
do fo, and I weep . . . Am I not a fool? . . .
I can't help it. . . . I pour out floods of tears to
think what human ceremonies have coft all
mankind, and particularly what a dreadful price
my native country has paid for them—and I
                                                        wifh

wifh with Luther, that there were no feaft-days among Chriftians, except the Lord's day. All Chriftians are not of our opinion. Some think the obfervation of this day a duty of religion. Very well. I wifh to be inftrufted. Permit me to fee how the duty is difcharged.

The far greater part of the members of the. eftablifhed church pay no regard at all to Good-Friday, nor do fome of them know why it is appointed. There is no piety furely in profeff-ing a religion, whioh is neither underftood nor obeyed. The greater part of opulent members of this community pay no other attention to the day than dining on fifh in preference to flefh. This is not piety. Numbers of the clergy read the ritual, and deliver a fermon compofed by others, and this is their whole performance. Moft artificers, and people of the lower clafs, imitate their fuperiors. Some of them do not obferve the day at all, and others, who hate work worfe than witchcraft, go in the morning to church, and in the evening to the alehoufe, and there depofite piety till Eafter Sunday, and then travel the fame round again. Should a man lay afide fecular affairs, abftain from food, drefs in black, go to church, fay after the parfon, hear the fer-mon, and clofe the day without company and cards, who but a methodift would pretend to ar-

raign

reign the conduct of this man? And yet, moſt certain it is, he may do all theſe without performing one act of genuine piety.

In ſhort, there are two general parents of religious action, cuſtom and conſcience. The firſt terminates, and produces a blind, ſordid, ſorry, crawling luſus, denominated religion; but really ſuperſtition. The latter, conſcience, may be enervated by ignorance, ſloth, ſcrupuloſity and ſecular intereſt, and in this ill ſtate of health may produce a weak family of genuine moral virtues, and of ſilly deformed ſuperſtitions: but, being right in the main, ſhe will always pay her firſt and chief attention to her moral offspring. Poſitive inſtitutes, and even human inventions, may be obeyed by people of this kind; but they will never encroach on the rights of natural, neceſſary, moral law. If the ceremonial of religion ſupply the place of religion itſelf—if the former derogate from the latter—if the former divert the attention from the latter—it becomes a reprehenſible ſuperſtition.

What then ſhall we ſay of thoſe, whoſe whole piety lies in the obſervation of *days, and times, and years?* We know what an inſpired apoſtle ſaid to ſuch people, *I am afraid I have beſtowed upon you labour in vain.* Father of univerſal nature! in vain haſt thou given us capacity, learn-

D　　　　ing.

ing, reafon, and religion—in vain does the knowledge of all antiquity fhine around us—in vain has the law of nature been explained to us by the writers of revelation—in vain haft thou beftowed thy beft and richeft gift the gofpel on us, and a government that allows us to judge of it—We live in the open violation of all thy laws—we curfe and fwear and blafpheme—we profane thy holy fabbaths—we are guilty of drunkennefs, debauchery, perjury, fimony, bribery, impiety, and irreligion of all kinds—our children are uneducated in religious principles —our property is wafted in gaming and amufements—our priefts and our prophets exemplify luxury—and we expect to avert all our deferved miferies, and to atone for all our impieties, by faying, have we not fafted on Good-Friday, and feafted on Eafter Sunday? The Jewifh priefts, at the worft of times, prophefied for hire; but fome Chriftian priefts take the hire and prophecy not. They vote indeed! but fay, ye plundered Nabobs! ye French Canadian Papifts! ye widows and orphans! ye depopulated cities, and ruined commerce of rebellious colonifts! fay, for what do Britifh minifters of the prince of peace vote? . . . . They vote that yon wheelwright's children muft faft on Good-Friday! This leads us to the laft article,

The POLITY of Good-Friday.

Before Chriftianity was underftood in the world, the firft apologifts for it *thought themfelves happy*, as St. Paul expreffes it, when they were called to defend it before equitable civil magiftrates in courts of legal judicature. They had great reafon to rejoice in thefe opportunities, for they taught a religion, which recommended itfelf to all juft governments by its perfect agreement with civil polity. Primitive Chriftianity wanted only to be known, it was fure to gain ground by being underftood. Thefe divine men were able to fay—Is the origin of civil government facred? We teach, that civil government is ordained by God.—Is the well-being of the whole the fupreme law in civil polity? So it is in Chriftianity.—Do ftates flourifh, when the people yield a ready obedience to civil government, and venerate the dignity of magiftracy? Chriftianity inculcates this.—Do temperance, induftry, piety, and virtue render ftates happy? Chriftianity forcibly inculcates thefe. —Are ftates happy when difcords do not prevail, when kind offices abound among citizens, when benevolence and philanthropy pervade the whole? Chriftianity abolifhes party factions and odious

diftinc-

diftinctions, and curbs the paffions that produce
them ; and as to univerfal love it is the religion
of Jefus itfelf.—Do ftates enjoy tranquillity when
learning and liberty, confcience and virtue are
nourifhed, and when impartial equity rewards
merit, and reftrains and punifhes vice ? Chriftianity does all thefe.—Are ftates fafe, when they
retain a conftitutional power of redreffing griev-
ances, of infuring life, liberty, and property from
foreign and domeftic invafion, and of reducing
all cafes to one invariable ftandard of impartial
and univerfal juftice ? Chriftianity inculcates
principles productive of all this. No inftance
therefore can be produced of our attempting to
fubvert civil government ; on the contrary, we
are entrufted with a conciliating plan of univerfal peace between fecular and facred things by
Jefus Chrift.

The corruptors of Chriftianity deprived it of
this noble plea ; they bartered purity for power,
exchanged argument for authority, and made a
fcandalous truck of all the truths and virtues of
religion for the feals of a prince, and the keys of
a goal. They invented words of inexplicable
myftery, and inflicted penalties on thofe, who
could not interpret their dreams—they caft in-
numerable canons, and with them deftroyed
the lives, and liberties, and properties of their
peaceable

peaceable brethren—they armed priefts with fecular power, and covered their barbarous ufe of
it with infinite pomp—they excited princes to
hate, perfecute, banifh, and burn their fubjects
for matters of confcience—they thought lay fubjects beneath notice, kings above law, and themfelves above kings. To their conduct it is ow-
ing, that moft great men confider religion as nothing more than an engine of ftate.

We hope Chriftianity in time will recover
from thefe deadly wounds : but healing and
health muft never be expected from fuch pre-
fcriptions as are made up of the falfe principles
that produced the hurt. The great, the only
object of fuch books as Hooker's church-polity,
and Gibfon's codex, is the fupport of the hierarchy. God knows, no pofitions can be lefs true,
no principles more dangerous than thofe laid
down in thefe compilations. Civilians fufficiently
fee'd could build the whole fabric of popery on
them; for the evident drift of them is not only to
render the church independent on the ftate; but
to place the ftate in a condition of dependence on
the church. Their fyftem is falfe in itfelf—in-
confiftent with Scripture—incompatible with the
Britifh conftitution—and deftructive of Chrift's
fpiritual defign. Thefe writers have lodged their
fentiments in the dark caverns of metaphorical
ftyle,

ftyle, and there they lurk in feeming afylum.
There is an imaginary being called the *church*
governing diftinct from the church governed—
this animal has *fex*, in violation of the Englifh
language, and the laws of precife argumenta-
tion—*She* is either married or a proftitute, for
fhe is a *mother*, it feems, and has children—All
this may be rhetorick; but nothing of this is
reafon, lefs ftill can it be called religion, and
leaft of all is it that religion which Jefus taught,
and which never diminifhes the glory of civil
polity.

The religion of Jefus is the moft fimple thing
in the world. His church was not formed on
the plan of the Jewifh government, either of
the ftate, temple, fanhedrim, or fynagogue—
nor on that of any other ftate, either that at
Rome, or that at Athens.—The decree of the
chriftian church at Jerufalem, called by miftake
the *firft council*, was advice; but not law.—Canons in the primitive church were opinions
devoid of coercion; the emperor Juftinian
adopted them, and metamorphofed them into
civil law—there were in the primitive church
no coercive powers—particular churches were
united only by faith and love—in all civil affairs
they were governed by civil magiftrates, and in
facred matters they were ruled by the advice,

reafons,

reasons, and exhortations of their freely elected officers—their censures were only honeft reproofs, and their excommunications were nothing more than declarations that the offenders were incorrigible, and were no longer accounted members of their focieties—the term *hierarchy* was unknown, and *hierodulia* would have been the proper defcription then—It was a fpiritual *kingdom not of this world*; it did not injure, it could not poffibly injure found civil polity. The primitive chriftians were taxed with holding feditious principles: and this calumny they merited for not getting drunk on Cæfar's birth-day—for holding their religious affemblies in the night, when fecular bufinefs was over—for refufing to fwear by the genius of Cæfar—for fcrupling to give him the titles that belonged to God—for talking of a kingdom of faints upon earth—however, thefe fons of fedition prayed for Cæfar—taught all due obedience to him—paid his tribute—fought in his wars—treated all inferior magiftrates with profound refpect; and thefe things they did not for prudential reafons of worldly policy, but from examined and adopted principles of genuine chriftianity.

The whole farrago of a fecular religion is a burden, an expence, a diftrefs to Government, and every corrupt part and parcel of it is fome
way

way or other injurious to civil polity. Confider
a kingdom as one large family, fum up the
prieftbood into one domeftic chaplain, compare
what he cofts with the good he does, and judge
whether the family gains as it ought, or lofes as
it ought not by his chaplainfhip.

To come to the point. We apply thefe general ftriftures to one article, confifting of fafts,
feafts, and holidays. We divide thefe into five
claffes, and difcharge four of them. In the firft
we place all thofe *obfolete* holidays, which were
in vogue before the Reformation, fuch as the
Affumption—the Conception—Silvefter—Britius
—and fuch like, which were very properly re-
tained in the calendar at the Reformation for
law ufes, for the afcertaining of the times of
tenures, and of the payment of dues—or of
charitable donations, that were dated by thefe
days. In a fecond clafs we put all the *Sundays*
in the year; for although fome divines hold the
morality of the Sabbath, and others place it
among pofitive inftitutes, yet all agree in the
neceffity of keeping a day, and a pious clergy
know how to improve it to the nobleft ufes of
church and ftate. In a third we put all *red-letter
days*, as coronation days, birth days, and others.
The fufpending of bufinefs on thofe days is a
very proper compliment to our civil governors,
and

and the healths and fpirits of gentlemen confined in public offices require relaxation and exercife. Nobody pretends to make religion of thefe, and they are on many accounts quite neceffary. In a fourth clafs we put all thofe *Saint's days*, and other holidays, which the clergy are obliged by their fuperiors to obferve. They ought not to complain, if they are required to faft on the 30th of January for the expiation of a crime, which nobody alive committed; for they are amply rewarded by many a feftival, from which none but themfelves ever derived the leaft benefit. All thefe we difmifs, and retain only a fifth fort of holidays, which conftitution and cuftom engage the whole national church to obferve; the fmalleft number of thefe is TEN. A very little attention will convince us, that the obfervation of thefe ten holidays is productive of no real advantage; but, on the contrary, of much damage to the nation at large.

As thefe feftivals are generally obferved, they hurt the healths, the morals, and the little property of the poor—they deprefs virtue, encourage vice, and generate fuperftition—they clog bufinefs, burden the clergy, increafe the rates of parifhes, endanger the peace of the fociety at large, perplex magiftrates—in a word, they impove-

E   rifh.

rifh the kingdom in proportion to the extent of their influence.

To examine only one of thefe articles: Suppofe a day labourer employed all the year at feven fhillings a week, that is, at fourteen pence a day; ten days of his time are worth to his family eleven fhillings and eight pence. Not to earn is to pay, and this poor fellow is actually at the annual charge of eleven and eight pence for the fupport of feftivals. Let us fuppofe farther, that his wife earns fix pence a day, and his four children four pence each, at fpinning, ftone-gathering, or any other work; ten days of the woman's time are worth five fhillings; ten days of each child are worth three and four pence. So that this man's wife and children pay for feftivals eighteen fhillings and four pence a year. We are farther to add the extraordinary expences of this family on thefe days; for it is all a farce to talk of their fafting, they have no fafts in their calendar, all are feftivals with them, and they never faft when they can get victuals. We allow the poor man, then, one fhilling on each day to fpend at the alehoufe, and his family one more for tea, beer, nuts, gingerbread and fo on. We are to add then twenty fhillings more to his account, and his reckoning ftands thus :

To

	£.	s.	d.
To 10 days work at 1s. 2d. each	0	11	8
To 10 days ditto of wife, at 6d. -	0	5	0
To 10 days ditto of four children,			
at 4d. each per day - -	0	13	4
To 10 days extra expences for self			
and family, at 2s. per day -	1	0	0
Total	2	10	0

Is not the fum of fifty fhillings enormous for this family, a heavy tax paid for a cargo of idlenefs! Let us fuppofe this poor man to enter thoroughly into the pretended defign of the day, to abftain from food as well as work, to faft and pray, and fpend nothing, ftill the faft cofts him all the money that he avoids earning, and this fimple devotee would pay twenty or thirty fhillings a year for the privilege of emaciating himfelf.

But the people derive great advantages from feftivals! . . . Good God! is religion magick! What people derive advantages from feftivals? they, who never attend them? It is notorious the poor are not to be found at church on Eafter and Whitfun-holidays. Enquire for the London populace at Greenwich, and for the country poor at the fign of the Crofs Keys. To fay they might reap

E 2   benefits,

benefits, and they ought to pay for the liberty, is equal to saying, the sober populace might get drunk at the Dog and Duck, and they ought to pay the reckoning of thofe who do.

Whatever advantages they derive from church-holidays, many of their neighbours derive great difadvantages from their finking fifty fhillings annually to fopport them. This poor fellow fhould pay thirty fhillings a year rent for his cottage; but the landlord never gets it, yet he would thank him to pay his rent by ten days work for him. He can pay no rates to the parifh, nor any taxes to government; yet were he allowed to earn fifty fhillings a year more than he does, he could pay both, and fave money to buy a pig, or a bullock, or firing too. He owes fome-thing to the doctor for phyfic, and fomething to the fhop for food, debts contracted in lyings-inn and illnefs, he can pay none of thefe drib-lets; yet he could pay all, were he allowed to earn fifty fhillings a year more, and to depofit it for payment of debts in his mafter's hands. Moreover, he got drunk on the feaft of the Epi-phany, which he called Twelfth night—fet up a fcore at the alehoufe—rolled in the dirt—fpoiled his clothes—loft his hat—fought with Sam Stride, who fent him a lawyer's letter, for which he paid fix and eight pence, befide a guinea to

Stride

Stride to make it up—and on the fame night he gave Blue Bridget nineteen pence for the liberty of leaving a baftard to the parifh—magiftrates were tormented with warrants, and oaths, and depofitions—peaceable fubjects with the interruptions of riot and debauchery—the whole bufinefs of the parifh ftood ftill—and the induftrious were obliged to pay out of their honeft gains the whole expence at laft.

What! it will be faid, would you keep thefe people in eternal employment, and allow them no holidays? I would keep them in perpetual employ. Six days they fhould labour, and do all they have to do, the feventh, being the fabbath of the Lord their God, the clergy fhould fo perform divine fervice as to engage them voluntarily to choofe to fill a religious affembly ; their children fhould be catechifed, and rational and agreeable pains fhould be taken to inftill the great principles of religion into them ; they fhould be taught a practice of piety, and a courfe of virtue; religion fhould be unmafked and expofed in its own beauty to their view; at prefent it appears to them an unmeaning encumbrance of expenfive forms. Their infants are queftioned, and fprinkled—their wives pay a fhilling and are churched.—they are generally funny at a wedding, and feel no expence but the ring—they

eat

eat crofs buns on Good-Friday—they are merry at Eafter—and mad at Chriftmas—they pay fmall tithes through life—and are buried in form when they die—and they call this the Chriftian Religion in the beft conftituted church in the world, and abufe all who think otherwife as knaves or fools, ignorant of God and difloyal to the king! As to holidays, let the poor take as many as they can afford, and their mafters can fpare. Far be it from us to wifh to abridge their liberty, or diminifh their little enjoyment of life: but let us not make religion of their gambols, nor enroll their paftimes among the laws of Jefus Chrift.

There were in the ritual of our anceftors above two hundred feftal days, many of them in feed-time, hay-time, and harveft. Great complaints were made to parliament; the church, it was faid, would ruin the ftate. While the people were telling beads, and the priefts chanting and fpouting away, the corn lay rotting in the fields, cattle were neglected, commerce was at a ftand, and the nation was ftarving. Legiflature ftruck off firft harveft-holidays, and then others, and what remain were left for a decoy to papifts, to the great grief of numbers, who fubmitted to them, and who wifhed to get rid of fuperftition, the root and the rind of popery.

If

If any imagine thefe feftivals neceflary for the
fake of informing people of the events that are
commemorated on them, and of preferving and
perpetuating the remembrance of them, we only
beg leave to afk—Where was Chriftianity fo well
underftood as in the primitive churches, which
celebrated none of them? Where is the Chriftian
religion lefs underftood than in the Roman community, where they are celebrated without end?
Who underftood Chriftianity beft, our Saxon
anceftors, who had many feftivals, or our im-
mediate parents, who had few? Is religion better
underftood in thefe reformed churches where
they are celebrated, than in thofe where they
are omitted? Does religion confift in the bare
remembrance of a few events in the life of Jefus
Chrift? May not all the ends propofed by the
obfervation of church-holidays be better anfwered
without it? Do we not facrifice many great advantages, and put ourfelves to unneceflary in-
conveniences and expences for mere fhadows,
which can never be fubftantiated without civil
coercion? Is not the likelieft method to make
the clergy loath the neceflary parts of their
office, the obliging of them to drudge alone in
unneceflary exercifes?—Many articles are omitted—under-rated—and half reafoned—but we
have

have said enough—perhaps too much—on the
ill polity of Good-Friday.

Should any parish priest of genuine and generous piety (for to sycophants and bigots we
have nothing to say) who loves God, reveres
his king, wishes well to his country and to all
mankind, should such a man say, I mourn for
the vices and calamities of my country, and I
dread those chastisements of Providence, which
national sins deserve... I wish to contribute my
mite to the publick good; but I know no better
way of promoting it than by inculcating the ob-
servation of fasts and feasts, and approved rituals.
I would venture to say to him,

Reverend Sir! I give you credit for being a
man too wise to quibble about style, where matters of the highest importance are in hand, and
too good to be offended with the honest blunt-
ness of one, whose reigning passion is to wish
felicity to all mankind. Pardon me, then, if I
take the liberty to say—The cool, disinterested
part of mankind consider a hierarchy as they
consider a standing military force. In absolute
monarchies, where the main principle of the con-
stitution is that of governing by fear, an hierarchy
is essentially necessary to the despotism of the
prince; but in free states an hierarchy will always
justly be an object of jealousy. Hierarchical
powers

powers have found many a ftate free, and re-
duced each to flavery: but there is no inftance
of their having brought an inflaved ftate into
chriftian liberty. Your country, Sir, is the only
one in the univerfe, in which civil liberty is the
very end and fcope of the conftitution. You
fhould therefore acquaint yourfelf well with all the
fingular polity of this country, which is governed
by a fyftem of laws all tending to the one great
defign, civil liberty, and you fhould not put off
the man, the citizen, and the chriftian, when
you put on the clerical character.—You profefs
a religion, Sir, which agrees with civil polity;
you know how fome of your order have deprived
it of this glory by refifting or duping their civil
governors in order to aggrandize themfelves.
Recover that character to Chriftianity, which
thofe crimfon tools of a defperate caufe, Auftin
and Lanfrank, Dunftan and Anfelm, Thurftan
and Becket, Longchamp and Peckham, Arundel
and Chichley, Woolfey and Bonner, Parker
and Whitgift, Bancroft and Laud, have vilely
fquandered away. Leave fecular affairs to fecular men. Have no more to do with commiffions
of the peace, county elections, commiffions for
roads, the civil affairs of hofpitals, corporations,
and fo on, than what you cannot poffibly avoid.
You may have rights as a gentleman; but it is

F   not

not neceffary you fhould lay afide the character
of a clergyman for the fake of afferting them.
Civil government adminiftered by clerical men
always infpires the lay gentry with jealoufy, and
the poor with contempt. In your office, be no
afpiring ftatefman's tool for filthy lucre's fake.
Do not dare to lift your unhallowed hand againft
the fovereign's title to the crown, and the people's right to liberty, by brandifhing the obfolete
and execrable doctrines of paffive obedience,
non-refiftance, the divine rights of kings, and
all the unconftitutional pofitions, which the
fupreme legiflature configned to eternal oblivion
at the glorious Revolution. Your fuperior may
put you on uttering what he dare not utter himfelf in order to feel the popular pulfe, and he
may procure interefted hirelings to applaud you,
and promife that preferment to you, which he
intends for himfelf. If you perifh in the attempt,
what cares he? But do not deceive yourfelf.
The prefent royal family will never prefer men
of arbitrary and unconftitutional principles. His
majefty perfectly comprehends the Britifh conftitution, and as he magnanimoufly afpires at
the glory of reigning over a free people, who
have confidence in his wifdom and goodnefs, it
is impoffible he fhould fmile on thofe, who lay
the ax to the root, the conftitution, and would
by

by one fatal blow fell thofe admired branches
his title and his people's liberties. Stir up no
ftrife in your public preaching, nor teach your
parifh to abhor an inhabitant of it for praying in
a barn. Never perfecute for religion's fake.
Never opprefs confcience. Never difcounte-
nance piety in other communities, left men
fhould think you not a minifter of religion, but
a tool of a party. Never condemn denomina-
tions in the grofs, nor impute principles and
practices to them, which they abhor. Sow no
jealoufies and difcords in families. Cultivate the
general principles of Chriftianity more than the
peculiarities of your own party, and the rights
of all mankind rather than the ritual of a very
inconfiderable part of them.—You are the minifter of a religion famous for its morality. Do
nothing to weaken this evidence of its divinity.

Avoid all grofs vices, drunkennefs, adultery,
lying, blafphemy, fabbath-breaking. It is not
enough for you to abftain from fwearing and
lying, you muft not take the Lord's name in
vain, nor allow yourfelf to prevaricate. Abftain
from what Scripture calls *filthinefs of fpirit*, pride,
levity, hypocrify, avarice, difcontent, diftruft,
mental immoralities. Practife all the moral
duties of both tables, and let your flock fee as
well as hear your doctrine. Have no fellowfhip
with

with thofe unfruitful works of darknefs, gaming, horfe-racing, frequenting taverns and alehoufes, play-houfes, opera-houfes, balls, affemblies, mafquerades; avoid alfo hunting, fhooting, dangling at the heels of Sir Robert, cringing at the levee of my lord, and fetching and carrying for my lady, of all which, whatever may be faid for fecular men, not one can be proper for you. The minifter of Chrift muft at leaft appear to be a man of delicate and refined moral virtue.— You are a minifter of a revealed religion. Study the Holy Scriptures, diftinguifh the doctrines of revelation from the difcoveries of philofophers ; the precepts of Chrift from the prudential faws of Epictetus; the doctrines and laws of his kingdom from human creeds and worldly maxims, and do not imagine that claffics and mathematics, novels, and plays, contain a body of chriftian divinity. Never turn the facred truths of revelation into ridicule, nor call *being born again, fearing the Lord, praying by the fpirit*, the cant of a party. The phrafeology of Scripture may have been mifunderftood; but you fhould not difcard both comment and text; you have adopted the book, and you ought to explain its meaning. Avail yourfelf of all opportunities of diffeminating Scripture knowledge. Catechize the children, and the poor in your parifh.

Carry

Carry religion home to their bofoms. Lay afide the felf-important haughtinefs of a prieft, and put on the meek and humble temper of your Mafter. Go into the cottages of the poor. Encourage their meeting together to pray and to read the Holy Scriptures. Teach them to fet up family worfhip, to perform a courfe of domeftic devotion, and, above all things, never countenance the profanation of the Lord's day, but teach them to reverence and improve it.— You are, Sir, a minifter in a rich community. Your country gives you good wages, and they expect at leaft fome work. Employ your emoluments to better purpofes than thofe of drefs and equipage, Sunday vifits, midnight revels, affemblies, fimoniacal contracts, and fuch like. Deteft the miferable difpofition of hoarding wealth, and dread being poffeffed with the rage of rifing to preferment. Remember, all church emoluments are fiduciary, and they lapfe into the public hand, when the fervices for which they were granted, are not performed. Flatter the vices of no patron ; but with a modeft boldnefs reprove them. Dare to be upright. Defpife the fhame of fingularity. Touch no fine-cures. Renounce needlefs pluralities. Do not plead for non-refidence, and, if you muft have a curate, let him fhare both work and wages.—It would

be

be tedious to you, were I to go through the duties that are annexed to all offices' from the curate up to the metropolitan of all England, and I will only beg your patience, while I add, in general, avoid the six vices, that difgrace too many of your order—deftroy the prejudices of deifts and infidels—allow, at leaft, the probability of fome defection—and adopt the courfe pre-fcribed by the oracles of God.

The principal vices that difgrace the prieft-hood are: 1. *Ignorance* of a body of Chriftian divinity. 2. *Perjury*, if they fubfcribe upon oath their belief of propofitions, which they have either not examined, or do not believe. 3. *Am-bition*, expreffed in a haughty referve in private life, a vain and pompous parade in public, a pedantic affectation of wifdom of words in their public preaching, by which they facrifice the edification of a whole congregation to the filly vanity of fhining as men of genius. 4. Infatia-ble *avarice*, ten thoufand times more tenacious of a four-penny Eafter-offering than of all the ten commandments. 5. *Time-ferving*, always pur-fuing thofe meafures which ferve their own in-tereft, furrendering to it philofophy and divi-nity, the intereft of their country and the honor of their God. 6. *Hypocrify*, acting a part, re-commending Chriftianity by office, and eftablifh-ing

ing paganifm by inclination, at church in maf-
querade, and at a play in their native character.
Such priefts as thefe turn the heavenly manna
into poifon. They give the enemies of religion
caufe to blafpheme, they are the ridicule of
Atheifts, and the reafons of Deifm! Be it your
holy ambition, Sir, to wipe off the foul prejudices
that defile the face of a weeping reformed
church. Your community is fufpected of fym-
bolizing with popery, for Parpalio the Pope's
nuncio offered in the Pope's name to confirm
your fervice-book. All reformed divines own,
the diftinguifhing characters of that apoftate
church are *three*, fuperftition, tyranny, and im-
morality. . Are there no evidences of your pof-
feffing thefe gloomy marks of Antichriftia-
nifm? Are your morals incorrupt? Do you
place no religion in habits, places, words,
and forms? Have you refigned the unrigh-
teous dominion over confcience, that in lefs
inquifitive times your order unjuftly acquired?
Have you like other penitents joined refti-
tution to repentance? Have you expelled no
ftudents for praying and reading the Scriptures?
denied ordination to no candidates on account
of their holding the doctrines of your own articles? fufpended and perfecuted no clergymen for
preaching more zealoufly than yourfelves? Have
you

you awed none into filence, who would fpeak
if they dare? What faid you to your petitioning
colleagues? and what to the diffenting clergy,
whom you flatter, and foothe, and call brethren
in Chrift? Are they freed from oaths, and fub-
fcriptions, and penal laws? Chriftian liberty!
thou favourite offspring of heaven! thou firft-
born of Chriftianity! I faw the wife and pious
fervants of God nourifh thee in their houfes, and
cherifh thee in their bofoms! I faw them lead
thee into public view! All good men hailed
thee! The generous Britifh Commons careffed
and praifed thee, and led thee into an upper
houfe, and there .... there didft thou expire
in the holy laps of fpiritual Lords! .... Allow, it is not impoffible, it is not improbable, it
is very likely, that MAY have happened in Chriftianity, which has happened in law; multifa-
rious ftatutes have obfcured plain common law.
Changing the term law for divinity, I will re-
cite the words of one of the chief ornaments of
that profeffion. The Chriftian religion has
fared like other venerable edifices of antiquity,
which rafh and unexperienced workmen have
ventured to new drefs and refine with all the
rage of modern improvement: hence frequently
its fymmetry has been deftroyed, its proportions
diftorted, and its MAJESTIC SIMPLICITY exchang-

5   ed

ed for specious embellishments and fantastic no-
velties. For, to say the truth, all niceties and
intricacies owe their original not to Scripture
divinity, but to additions and innovations, often
on a sudden penned by men, who had none, or
very little judgment in divinity. . . . . In fine,
Sir, feed the flock of God, which he hath pur-
chafed with his own blood—Covet no man's
silver, or gold, or apparel—Warn every one
night and day with tears—Serve the Lord with
all humility of mind—Keep back nothing that is
profitable to us—Teach us publicly, and from
houfe to houfe—Teftify to Jews and Greeks neither worldly politics, nor human inventions,
but repentance toward God, and faith in our
Lord Jefus Chrift—Watch in all things—Do the
work of an evangelift—Make full proof of your
miniftry—Give attendance to reading, to exhor-
tation, to doctrine—Meditate upon thefe things
—Give thyself wholly to them.—Do thefe
things, and then, when you are become venera-
bly hoary in the beft of fervices, finifh your
courfe with joy—take Britain and her colonies,
proteftantifm and popery, Canada and China,
your own church and other reformed churches,
heaven and earth, to record that you are pure
from the blood of all men—Quit the world like
your divine Mafter, and afcend to heaven, you

G   bleffing

. bleffing us, and we admiring you. . . . . But
if, on the contrary, neglecting all the duties of
your office, and practifing all the vices that ever
provoked the patience of God and man—If you
enter the church by that door, by which Ana-
nias was turned out, profeffing to be moved by
the Spirit of God, while you are actuated only
by ambition or avarice—If fo far from coming
up to the fpirit of thofe qualifications, which are
required to ordination, you fall fhort of the very
letter, either in learning, morality, or knowledge of theology—If you fubfcribe thirty-nine
articles, three creeds, the genuine and the apo-
cryphal Scriptures, the books of prayer, ordination, and homilies, and fwear canonical obedience to one hundred and forty-one canons, without having read, examined, and believed the
whole—If you take the oath of fupremacy, and
hold, that the church hath legiflative power—
If you abjure Popery upon oath, and yet hold the
principal articles that fupport it—If you fwear al-
legiance to his Majefty, and teach anti-revolutional
principles—If you obtain preferment by fimony
direct or indirect—If you take charge of 2000
fouls, and never fpeak to 1900 of them—If you
hold contradictory doctrines while you profefs uniformity—If you have a catechifm, and
never teach it—If you neglect your duty to hunt
                                          after

after preferment —If you enjoy the emoluments of a fpiritual office in perfon, and do the fervices of it by proxy—If you hate reformation, and depreciate and perfecute thofe who would reform you —If you mifreprefent peaceable fubjects, taxing them with herefy, fchifm, and republicanifm, and ftrive to render their loyalty to the crown, and their love to the conftitution doubtful—If you profane Sabbaths, and ordinances of divine appointment—If all your ftudy is to make a fair fhew in the flefh—If you mind only earthly things, your god being your belly, and glorying in your fhame—and vainly imagine to cover all thefe crimes by obferving a Good-Friday, and fo to gull mankind into a perfuafion of your fapience and fanctity—know of a truth—the time may come, when your civil governors may fee it as neceffary to reform your reformation as their anceftors did to reform the religion of your predeceffors—till then, although the religion of pious fpectators will not fuffer them to hurt a hair of your head, yet the fame religion will oblige them to fay of you—This evil man talks of light, while his feet are ftumbling on dark mountains—his country and the fmall remains of his own confcience, the canons of his church and the laws of the ftate, the liberalities of his prince and the tears of his brethren, the

2   afhes

aſhes of Burnets and Hoadleys and Lardners, the juſt judgments of heaven on degenerate prieſts and incorrigible nations, all call him to his duty, and warn him of the danger of falling into the hands of an angry God—if he will not hear, our ſouls ſhall weep in ſecret places for his ignorance and pride.

F I N I S.

www.ingramcontent.com/pod-product-compliance
Lightning Source LLC
Chambersburg PA
CBHW021231260626
47172CB00002B/713